P9-CRX-347

The Clue in the
Painted Pattern

**Written & Illustrated
by Ken Bowser**

Solving Mysteries Through
Science, Technology, Engineering, Art & Math

**RED
CHAIR
•PRESS•**

Egremont, Massachusetts

The Jesse Steam Mysteries are produced and published by:
Red Chair Press LLC   PO Box 333   South Egremont, MA 01258-0333
www.redchairpress.com

FREE Educator Guide at www.redchairpress.com/free-resources

For My Grandson, Liam

Publisher's Cataloging-In-Publication Data
Names: Bowser, Ken, author, illustrator.
Title: The clue in the painted pattern / written & illustrated by Ken Bowser.

Description: South Egremont, MA : Red Chair Press, [2020] | Series: A
    Jesse Steam mystery | "Solving Mysteries Through Science, Technology,
    Engineering, Art & Math." | Includes a makerspace activity for hands-on
    learning about art and patterns. | Summary: "While on a camping trip,
    Jesse finds a curious piece of stone with an interesting pattern on it.
    With research, and the help of Professor Peach, she learns that it's a
    piece of broken pottery with a pattern unique to a certain Native
    American tribe. After an archeological dig with the Professor and her
    friends, she finds more pieces of the ancient artifact. Using her art
    skills, Jesse is able to preserve the clay pot."--Provided by publisher.

Identifiers: ISBN 9781634409513 (library hardcover) | ISBN 9781634409520
    (paperback) | ISBN 9781634409537 (ebook)

Subjects: LCSH: Indian pottery--Juvenile fiction. | Art and design--
    Juvenile fiction. | Pottery, Ancient--Conservation and restoration--
    Juvenile fiction. | CYAC: Indian pottery--Fiction. | Design--Fiction. |
    LCGFT: Detective and mystery fiction.

Classification: LCC PZ7.B697 Cl 2020 (print) | LCC PZ7.B697 (ebook) | DDC
    [Fic]--dc23

LC record available at https://lccn.loc.gov/2019936020

Printed in the United States of America

0520 1P CGF20

Table of Contents

Cast of Characters

Jesse Steam

Amateur sleuth and all-around neat kid. Jesse loves riding her bike, solving mysteries, and most of all, Mr. Stubbs. Jesse is never without her messenger bag and the cool stuff it holds.

Mr. Stubbs

A cat with an attitude, he's the coolest tabby cat in Deanville. Stubbs was a stray cat who strayed right into Jesse's heart. Can you figure out how he got his name?

Professor Peach

A retired university professor. Professor Peach knows tons of cool stuff and is somewhat of a legend in Deanville. He has college degrees in Science, Technology, Engineering, Art and Math.

Emmett

Professor Peach's ever-present pet, white lab rat. He loves cheese balls, and wherever you find The Professor, you're sure to find Emmett— even though he might be difficult to spot!

Clark & Lewis

Jesse's next-door neighbor and sometimes formidable adversary, Clark Johnson, and his slippery, slimy, gross-looking pet frog, Lewis. Yuck.

Dorky Dougy

Clark Johnson's three-year-old, tag-along baby brother. Dougy is never without his stuffed alligator, a rubber knife, and something really goofy to say, like "eleventy-seven."

Kimmy Kat Black

Holder of the Deanville Elementary School Long Jump Record, know-it-all, and self-proclaimed future member of Mensa. Kimmy Kat Black lives near the Spooky Tree.

Liam LePoole

A black belt in karate, and also the captain of the Deanville Community Swimming Pool Cannonball Team. Liam's best friend is Chompy Dog, his stinky, gassy, and frenzied brown Puggle.

Backwoods Brandi

Rugged outdoorswoman, camp counselor, occasional lifeguard, and keeper of the campfire. During the school year, Brandi's the gym coach at Deanville Elementary School.

The Scary Shadow

Who or what can be casting this scary, mysterious shadow on the walls of Jesse's and Kimmy Kat Black's cabin? Can you guess? Keep reading and find out!

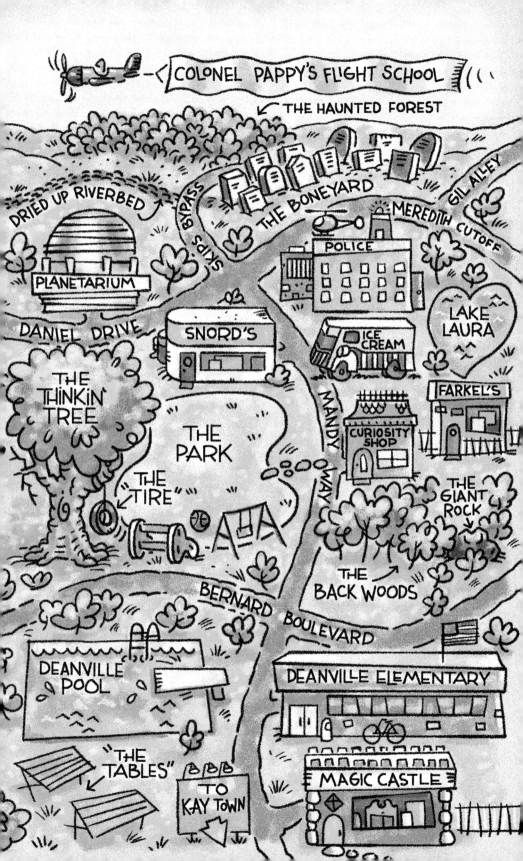

A Giant Trunk, Some Special Tools and One Conniving Cat

Chapter 1

It was a hot summer afternoon, and the sun beamed in through Jesse's window like a gold doubloon. "Ahh!" she said to Mr. Stubbs. "It's the first day of summer break, and I'm ready for a full week in the great outdoors." Stubbs glanced at her smugly with one eye open as he slept in the sunbeam.

"Ahead of me lie seven exhilarating days and six tranquil nights at beautiful Camp Tealahatchee without a care in the world," she told the lazy cat. "Too bad ya can't go with me, old man," Jesse teased. "Just hang here with the fam, and I'll be back before ya know it. Stay out of trouble, and maybe I'll bring you a surprise."

Jesse lifted the heavy lid on her camp trunk and began sorting through all of the things she needed to pack for her week-long excursion. "Well, let's see here, Stubby Dude," she said to the still-snoozing cat. "Besides boots, and sleeping bags, and the normal camp stuff, I think I'll add a few extra items to my trusty old messenger bag." Jesse never went anywhere without her bag. It contained all of the things any amateur sleuth would need to solve great puzzles and mysteries.

"Along with the other things I always keep in my bag, like my spyglass, my disguise, and my journal and stuff, I'm going to bring a small shovel, a pick, and some other archaeological tools," she explained. "Being out in the forest for a week presents a terrific opportunity for me to do some excavating for fossils, rocks, and minerals. Maybe I'll even find an old Spanish coin! Guess I can't bring my favorite blanket," she said kind of sadly. Even though she was excited about going, this was Jesse's first

time at sleepaway camp, so she was also kind of apprehensive. "Oh well," she sighed.

Jesse turned away to place the blanket back in her drawer. "Like I said, Stubbs. You behave while I'm gone, and I'll bring you something back from camp. Maybe some wild catnip or something," she joked. "Like you're not wild enough already." She laughed over her shoulder.

Turning back around, Jesse did not see Mr. Stubbs. Nor did she notice the fact that he had quietly slipped into her messenger bag. "Hey. Where'd ya go, Stubbs?" She looked around. "Guess he's at his food bowl. Stay out of trouble while I'm gone, Stubby!" she hollered to him as she slung the bag over her shoulder. "See ya!"

Jesse pushed her big trunk to the front door and got ready for the short two-hour ride to camp.

Kimmy Kat Black Hops in the Back

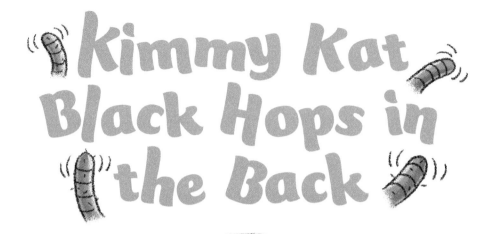

Chapter 2

Looking up from the driveway, Jesse wondered why Stubbs wasn't sitting in the front window, like he usually was when she was going somewhere. "Must be at his food bowl still," she guessed out loud. "He's a hungry little booger." She snickered.

With her camp trunk safely in the back of the van, Jesse hoisted her messenger bag over her shoulder again. *Man,* she thought to herself. *Is this thing heavier and bulkier than it should be? It must be the extra stuff I put in there. Oh well.*

Jesse climbed in the back seat. *Off we go,* she thought. She was still apprehensive about sleepaway camp. *At least Kimmy Kat Black will be with me.*

The van pulled down Byrd Street and rounded the corner at Perry Snord's Service

Station. "Kimmy Kat Black lives just around the corner by the Spooky Tree," she mumbled out loud. "I can't wait till she's here. I already miss Stubbs, and I could use some company."

They pulled up to Kimmy's house, and she hopped in after her trunk was placed in the back with Jesse's.

"Hey, Jesse gal," Kimmy smiled. "Ready for a week of fun and adventure?" she asked.

Kimmy Kat Black buckled her seatbelt and continued. "What's going on, cabin-mate?" she joked with Jesse. "Are we gonna have fun or what?" Jesse quickly forgot all about missing Stubbs, and she stopped being nervous about her first time at sleepaway camp.

"I've packed my birding journal, along with my binoculars," Kimmy said. "I plan on studying the flora and fauna of the surrounding area. That is, when I'm not beating all of the boys at running, and swimming, and softball and stuff," she boasted.

Kimmy Kat Black was the star of the Deanville Elementary School Track Team and was accustomed to beating the boys at every imaginable sport.

"I've packed some cool archaeological gear," Jesse said. "I studied topographical maps of the area all last week, and I learned that there's a dried-up riverbed on the camp grounds. I'm excited to do some excavating there," she went on.

"Neat," Kimmy Kat Black replied, seeming unimpressed.

"Who knows what those dumb old boys will be doing all week," Kimmy Kat said. "At least Clark won't be bringing his slimy frog Lewis. NO PETS ALLOWED is the rule at Camp Tealahatchee," she said.

"Thank goodness!" they both chimed. "They're in the cabin next to us. Pee-ew!" They grossed out together.

The van turned sharply onto bumpy

Tealahatchee Trail. The day grew late. The sun began to sink, and the forest began to darken a bit. "If I didn't have you here," Jesse said, "I'd be a little bit frightened." The van drove under a big timber sign. "Welcome To Camp Tealahatchee," the large sign read.

Bags and Trunks, Poison Ivy and a Mysterious Sound

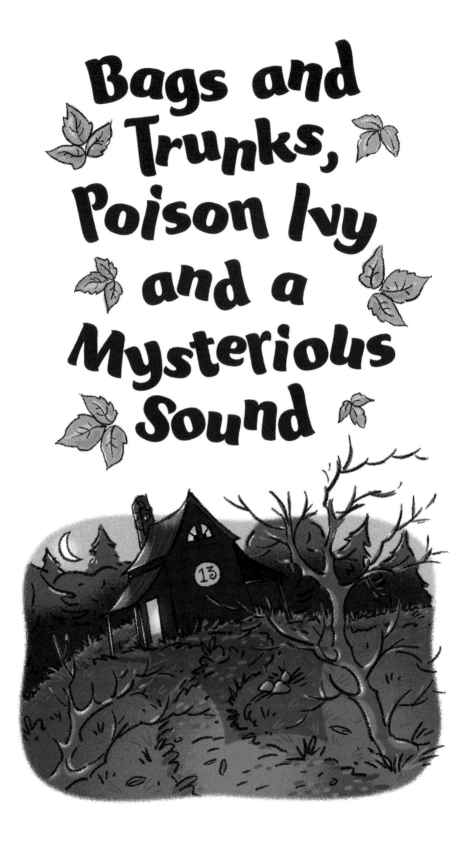

Chapter 3

The van rumbled up to the main camp cabin, and the two soon-to-be-campers were met by the camp counselor, Backwoods Brandi. "Howdy, campers!" she greeted the girls. "You must be Jesse Steam and Kimmy Kat Black," Counselor Brandi said as she flipped the pages on her clipboard.

"Yep! That's us," they answered in unison.

"Great to meet you! You guys are in cabin 13, just up the big hill and to the left," she pointed out. "Grab yer gear and get a move on. And don't dilly-dally. It'll be dark soon."

The girls looked at the path winding up the big hill, and then looked down at their bags and trunks. "Well, this doesn't look like much fun," Jesse groaned. They began to gather their things, as it was beginning to grow dark.

With their bags over their shoulders, Jesse and Kimmy Kat Black each took one end of the first trunk. "This is going to take two trips," Kimmy said.

"I think you're right," Jesse replied with a grunt as she lifted her end of the trunk. "It doesn't make it any easier with my bag across my shoulder, but I'm certainly not leaving it unattended anywhere."

After a lot of trudging and complaining, the two already-tired campers, finally dragged the first trunk into cabin 13. While they rested for a minute, they flipped a coin to see who got the top bunk. "Heads, it's yours," Jesse said as the coin spun to a stop on the floor beneath the bottom bunk. Then, as Jesse knelt down to retrieve the coin from far under the bed, she heard a strange sound. "RRRRR," it rumbled.

"Did you... you... you hear that, Kimmy?" Jesse worried.

"Huh? No. I didn't hear a thing." Kimmy shrugged.

"OK?" Jesse questioned nervously. "I guess it was just my imagination," she gulped.

"Hey, let's go get the last trunk before it gets any darker," Kimmy suggested.

Soon they were halfway back up the big hill with the last trunk. "I need to sit and rest for a while, Jesse," Kimmy said.

"I'm going to plop down here in the grass for a second." Jesse laid back with her arms behind her head and looked up at the sky. "Sure is a pretty night, Kimmy." The sky was still light enough to see a few bats were now fluttering about for dinner, and fireflies began to put on their evening light show.

"Uhhh, Jesse..." Kimmy Kat Black hesitated and said cautiously. "What's that you're lying on?"

"This stuff?" Jesse asked. "I don't know. Some kind of weed, I guess," she went on.

"Uhhh," Kimmy continued. "I'm pretty familiar with native flora, and if I didn't know better, I'd say you're laying on poison ivy, my friend," Kimmy said.

"Oh, just great!" Jesse jumped up. "All I need! Starting camp week with a case of poison ivy! Way to go, Jesse!" she scolded herself.

They picked up the trunk again and lugged it up the hill. "Let's look in my plant books as soon as we get settled," Kimmy said.

Back in the cabin, Kimmy studied her books. "Well, you're in luck," Kimmy Kat Black said to Jesse. "While it looked just like poison ivy," she continued, "it's not." Kimmy referred to her flora and fauna book. "Poison ivy has three leaves, and the small plants you were laying on had four, so you're OK." She read on. "Leaves of three, let it be. That's good advice," she said. "I'll remember that."

"It's getting pretty dark now," Jesse said. "Better get our flashlight lanterns out." Just as Kimmy was putting her book down, and before Jesse could get her lantern, the two sat up quickly.

"Jeeeessseee?" Kimmy Kat Black asked nervously. "Wha... wha... what was that noise?" she whimpered.

"That's that noise I heard earlier," Jesse

whispered. "Shhh! There it is again," she whispered.

"Mrrrrrrr," the weird noise sounded again. "Mrrrrrrr," it murmured from somewhere in the darkening room. The two girls were very still but moved closer to each other. They felt their hearts beating. They sat very quietly.

A Mysterious Sound, a Big Spooky Shadow and a Startling Surprise

Chapter 4

Jesse and Kimmy Kat Black scooted closer and closer to one another on the bunk as the scary, mysterious noise grew louder and closer. "Mrrrrrrr," it sounded again.

"What... Is... It...?" Kimmy Kat Black asked nervously, her teeth chattering.

"I don't know. I'm getting frightened," whispered Jesse anxiously.

"I want to go hoooome, Jesse!" Kimmy Kat Black said as the light from the moon shined in through the window.

"Wha... Wha... What is tha... tha... that?" Kimmy Kat Black trembled. Jesse looked up to see the frightening sight that had caught Kimmy's attention. Jesse grabbed Kimmy's hand as she saw a giant, spooky shadow being cast upon the wall.

"I want to go hooooome!" both girls

whimpered out loud together.

The spooky, shadowy shape on the wall grew bigger and bigger. The scary noise grew louder and louder. "Mrrrrrrrr. Mrrrrrrrr." The noise grew.

Suddenly and quickly, the shadow moved across the wall, and the girls felt something pounce down next to them heavily on the bunk.

"Aaaayyyy!" they both screamed. Jesse grappled for her flashlight and turned it on. When the flashlight illuminated the room, the girls could not believe their eyes.

"STUUUUUUBBS!" they both yelled in relief. "It was you on the windowsill all along! What are YOU doing here?" They howled with laughter at the cat.

Seashells & Shark's Teeth 100 Miles From the Ocean

Chapter 5

The next morning, Jesse and Kimmy Kat Black made up their bunks and prepared to go to the main cabin for breakfast. "Okay, listen here, Stubbs," Jesse scolded. "I'm not the least bit happy that you snuck into my bag, but there's nothing I can do about it now," she chided the naughty cat. "I have to go eat breakfast, and I'll bring you something back to eat, but it's important that you stay out of sight until I get back, or we're BOTH in big trouble! Got it?" she said sternly. Stubbs smiled, and purred, and curled up under Jesse's bunk for another morning nap.

Jesse and Kimmy Kat Black arrived to breakfast to find the usual gang seated at the big center table. Clark Johnson was there, but his slimy frog Lewis had to stay home. "I'll find another frog to hang out with while

I'm here." He laughed. "I would have brought Lewis with me," he said. "But you guys know the rules. NO PETS ALLOWED AT CAMP TEALAHATCHEE!" Clark announced.

Kimmy and Jesse's eyes widened as they looked at each other and winked. "Where's your little brother, Clark?" they asked.

"He's only here for day camp," Clark said. "Thank goodness. I sure don't need that little runt taggin' along too much."

During breakfast, they all talked about
the activities they were going to partake in
that day. "As soon as I finish scarfing down
these gnarly scrambled eggs, I'm going to go
to the archery course," Clark bragged to the
kids. Liam LePoole chimed in next.

"I'm going down to the dock to practice
my cannonballs. My mom always told me I
would make a big splash one day! I think she
was right!" he joked.

Jesse got back to the cabin and gave Stubbs a few bits of bacon and the carton of milk she saved from her breakfast. "That oughta hold ya till lunch," she told the hungry cat. "It looks like I'm stuck with you here, Stubbs, so you need to stick close to me everywhere I go. I don't want you getting into any mischief here in the cabin by yourself," she continued as he finished his breakfast. "C'mon. Climb in, buddy." Stubbs hopped into her bag, and off they went to explore.

As the two hiked down a trail, Jesse held a small topographical map of the area that she had copied out of a book at the library. "It says here, Stubbs, that there's a dried-up riverbed just at the end of this trail." Mr. Stubbs watched over her shoulder from her bag as they walked. "I think this would be a great place to start to dig around," she said.

Jesse and Stubbs got to the end of the trail and came to a small ravine that was just

a short distance from their cabin. "Let's try here," Jesse said.

After setting her bag down, she and Mr. Stubbs got situated and began to dig into the sandy soil looking for anything of interest. Before long, Jesse had accumulated a small pile of interesting rocks and stone fragments. "Look at this, old Stubby boy." She smiled at

the cat. "I wonder where this came from?" Jesse held up a small seashell. "We're a long, long way from the nearest ocean," she puzzled. She held up another small item. "And this looks like a shark's tooth. I've seen them in my books. I can't imagine how in the world these got here," she said, holding up her find.

"Now, what do you suppose this is, Stubbs?" Mr. Stubbs was stretched out on a big stone and lounging in the sun. Jesse held up a strange-looking rock. "I can't even imagine," she said with wonder as she held up what appeared to be a flat, orange stone. It had an interesting, jaggedy pattern on it. "I've never seen a rock like this," she said to Stubbs as she turned it over again and again in her hands. She tucked the stones into her bag. "C'mon, Stubbs. We better get back."

Chapter 6

Returning to the cabin, Jesse and Mr. Stubbs ran into Kimmy Kat Black as she was coming back from the softball field. "How was your day, Kimmy?" Jesse asked.

"Terrific, old pal!" Kimmy boasted. "I beat everyone at running, jumping, archery, and swimming! And I've got the trophies and medals to prove it." Kimmy held up the shiny medals that were around her neck. "How about you? How'd you make out on your rock hunt?" Kimmy asked.

"Minerals," Jesse replied.

"Huh?" Kimmy questioned.

"I was looking for minerals, too, not just rocks," Jesse continued.

"Oh. Yeah. Whatever." Kimmy Kat Black shrugged.

Back in the cabin, Kimmy and Stubbs

watched while Jesse spread her assortment
of rocks and minerals out on her bunk.

"Wow. Those really are cool," Kimmy
declared as Stubbs looked on. Then Jesse
held one up that looked almost like a
crystal that hung from the chandelier at her

grandmother's house.

"It says here in my *Rocks & Minerals Field Guide* that this is a quartz crystal. They're pretty common if you know where to look." Jesse handed the beautiful, clear crystal to Kimmy.

"Now, wanna see something really cool?" Jesse asked. "This is a shark's tooth and this is a seashell. My geology book tells me that millions of years ago, the very spot that we're sitting on, right this minute, was once covered by a vast ocean. There's no tellin' how old these things are!" she whispered with amazement.

Then Jesse held up the mysterious flat, orange rock with the jaggedy pattern on it. "This one has me really stumped," Jesse said with a perplexed look. "I can't find this stone in any of my books."

Jesse spent the rest of her week at Camp Tealahatchee working like a real geologist.

And the more cool stuff she found and shared, the more the other kids wanted to come and watch. "This is really neat, Jesse," Clark was heard to say. "I never knew you could find such cool stuff just digging around in the dirt." He laughed.

By the last day of camp, they had found more seashells—there were a lot of those. Kimmy Kat found another shark's tooth, and Jesse found another quartz crystal, but it wasn't as big or as nice as the first one she found. Dorky Dougy unearthed a gross hunk of dried-up chewing gum. "Not a rock, Dougy!" They all laughed.

Back at the cabin, they began to pack up for home. Jesse had amassed an impressive collection of interesting rocks and minerals, and she read about every one of them in her books. Except for one—the mysterious, flat, orange rock with the jaggedy pattern on it. That one was still a conundrum.

Professor Peach Ponders the Painted Pattern

Chapter 7

Mr. Stubbs was especially happy to be back home and sleeping in his own bed. Camp Tealahatchee was a great adventure—but not for a housecat.

Jesse spent two entire days cataloging her rocks and minerals. She even made an organizer for them out of some cardboard egg cartons. "These will keep them all in order," she explained to Mr. Stubbs. Then she created a chart that recorded where she found each one, along with their geological names, and pasted it into the inside of the top. She had chronicled each specimen. All but one. She still had no clue about the mysterious, flat, orange rock with the jaggedy pattern on it.

Jesse studied the mysterious rock again. She looked at it closely through her magnifying glass. She weighed it. She smelled it. She tapped on it. She flicked it with her fingernail. She even bit it. "Youch, that's hard!" She winced as she bit. Jesse pored through every rock and mineral book she could put her hands on, but she still could not find anything remotely similar to that mysterious rock in any source. "What in the world can this thing be?" she asked herself. Frustrated, Jesse stuffed the rock in her back pocket.

"I'm done racking my brain, Stubbs." She sighed. "Let's step away from this for a while and get some fresh air. We've been cooped up in here for two days tryin' to figure this thing out."

It was nice being outside. Mr. Stubbs was happy to be in the front basket of Jesse's bike again. They hadn't gotten far down Byrd Street when they heard Professor Peach.

"Hey there, Jesse." He waved. "Haven't seen you around lately."

"Yep," Jesse replied. "Been away at Camp
Tealahatchee for a whole week!"

"Now that's exciting, Jesse," the
Professor said. "What all did you do while
you were away?" he inquired.

"Mostly looked for neat rocks and
minerals," she replied.

"My, my!" the Professor said proudly. "We have a geologist in our midst, don't we, Mr. Stubbs?" He scratched Mr. Stubbs on the cheek. "What sort of things did you unearth, Jesse?"

She told him about the shells and the shark's teeth. She told him about the quartz crystal. And then, she told him about the mysterious, flat, orange rock with the jaggedy pattern on it. "I've looked in every rock and mineral book I can find, but I still can't figure out what it is," she said.

"Well, you'll have to show it to me one day." The Professor hoped. "Perhaps I can assist you in your quandary," he proposed. The Professor was always using weird words like *quandary*.

"I have it right here, Professor," Jesse said as she

pulled the rock from her back pocket. "Take a look."

"Ah, well, let me make a quick assessment." The Professor pulled a small, metal cylinder out of his top pocket. It was about an inch long with glass on both ends. "This is a jeweler's loupe, Jesse. It's a type of magnifying glass," he explained.

The Professor squinted his eye around the thing and held the rock up close. He studied the back. He studied the sides. And he looked very closely at the jaggedy pattern on the front.

"Oh, dear Jesse!" he exclaimed. "You're not only a geologist. You're an archaeologist too!" He chuckled. "This is not a rock or a mineral at all!" He laughed out loud. "This my dear," the Professor said, "is a fragment of an ancient piece of pottery! The first clue is this pattern. You see, it's painted on." Jesse looked closely at the object.

"Whooooa," she muttered softly under her breath.

"And according to my history books," the Professor went on, "the area that Camp Tealahatchee occupies now was once inhabited, hundreds of years ago, by a Native tribe of great artists and craftsmen."

I Can Dig it, He Can Dig it, She Can Dig it, We Can Dig it

Chapter 8

"Not a rock or a mineral at all! No wonder I couldn't find it in a book on rocks!" Jesse laughed.

"And what's more," the Professor went on, "if this piece was there, then there is a very good chance that there are more like it. We just might excavate additional pieces of that very same piece of pottery if we go about it methodically and scientifically," the Professor advised. "Now, gather up some of your friends, and tomorrow morning I'll show you kids how to go about conducting a genuine archaeological dig."

The next morning arrived, and Jesse and her friends were excited about their chances at working like real archaeologists. Liam LePoole was there, still sporting the medal he had won at camp for doing the most outrageous cannonball. Clark was there, of course, and so was his annoying, tag-along baby brother, Dorky Dougy. "I'm gonna be a ar-pa-la-la-gus," Dougy said.

"Not a word, Dougy!" They all laughed.

They left their bikes at the rack by the main cabin and made their way down the trail to the dried-up riverbed, where the Professor was already waiting.

"Kids," the kind, old Professor said, "the first thing we need to do is grid out the area in which we will be working."

"If we do this properly, we can excavate one small sector at a time and not miss anything significant," he went on. "We'll start here at the exact spot where Jesse found her first piece of pottery. We'll create a four-foot square grid and excavate that area a few inches down at a time."

The Professor showed the kids how to make a four-foot square grid with wooden stakes and some string. "Now," said the Professor, "we may proceed."

The kids used small shovels and began to gently dig a few inches of soil at a time. "Carefully place your soil into this tray one scoop at a time, kids," the Professor advised. The Professor had made a wooden frame with a screen at the bottom. "Once the sandy

soil is in the tray, we'll shake it through the screen and gather the larger fragments that remain in the tray so we can study them," he explained.

The Professor shook one tray at a time, and each tray revealed something new. More seashells, of course. Some small stones and then... "Another piece of pottery!" Jesse exclaimed. More soil through the screen produced more shells, and stones, and more and more pieces of pottery.

"Just as I suspected," the Professor deduced. "The area in which Jesse found the first piece yielded a plethora of additional pottery pieces." The Professor was always using words like plethora. When they finished, they had excavated the entire grid. "Now to backfill our site. We must leave the area just as pristine as we found it," he lectured.

Back at the Professor's front porch,

the kids went to work reassembling the fragmented pottery. "This is like a three-dimensional jigsaw puzzle," Kimmy Kat Black said.

"Yes, and if we work carefully and diligently, we'll be amazed at what we find," the Professor taught.

The kids worked for hours piecing and gluing each fragment together. "The pattern actually makes it easier to put it together correctly," Jesse observed.

When they were done, Jesse lifted the reassembled pot carefully in her hands. "Whooooa. An ancient Indian artifact," she whispered out loud to her friends, amazed.

"It's beautiful," the kids agreed.

"Now what are you going to do with it, Jesse?" the Professor asked.

"Keep it on my dresser?" she said.

"Well, that would be nice, but wouldn't you rather share it with everyone?" he questioned.

"Sure, I guess, but how?" Jesse asked. "We can't just take turns with it. It's too fragile to simply pass around like that." She worried.

"Well, I have an idea," the Professor said.

Jesse spent the rest of her summer studying Native American culture and the fascinating people who once inhabited the Deanville area hundreds of years before. "Just think, Stubbs," she said. "Hundreds of years ago, someone made this with their own two hands and used it in their everyday life," she said with amazement, as she carefully placed the piece of pottery in its new home. Mr. Stubbs didn't seem the least bit interested. "That was a great idea the Professor had about sharing it, don't you think, Stubby?" she asked.

The weather grew hot the next week as Jesse prepared for the first day of school. "Boy," she said to Stubbs. "Summer flew by, didn't it?" He looked at her with one eye.

Ancient American Indian Artifact
Excavated & donated by:
Jesse Steam.
Geologist and Archaeologist

"Now stay out of trouble while I'm gone, mister!" she warned. "I'll be home at the regular time."

When Jesse arrived at school, a small crowd had already gathered in front of the new display in the library. "Wow, Jesse!" one kid said. "You really discovered that?" he asked.

"Well, yeah." She laughed. "But I had a little help from a certain furry friend."

THE END

Jesse's Word List

Accumulated
when things pile up—like dirty dishes

Accustomed
to get used to something—*I got accustomed to my tight underwear.*

Cataloging
making a list—*She's cutting and cataloging her fingernails.*

Cautiously
do something carefully—like picking up a spider

Chided
to yell at someone—*Take the #@*! trash out!*

Conundrum
something really confusing—like pre-algebra

Doubloon
an old Spanish coin that pirates sometimes used

Excavate
to dig something out–like boogers

Exhilarating
scary and fun at the same time–like the hiccups

Frustrated
how you feel when something bugs you–like your teacher

Hoist
to lift up—*Help me hoist my stinky socks up.*

Howl
what you do when you stub your toe really hard

Inhabited
things living somewhere—*Flies inhabit the windowsill.*

Outrageous
something shocking—like when the kid in homeroom threw up

Plethora
a large amount—like hair in your uncle's ears

Quandary
not knowing what to do—like how you feel now

Ravine
a narrow gorge—like the space between sofa cushions

Trudge
to walk slowly—like when you're on your way to school

Unison
saying something all together—*We hate homework!*

About the Author & Illustrator

Ken Bowser is an illustrator and writer whose work has appeared in hundreds of books and countless periodicals. While he's been drawing for as long as he could hold a pencil, all of his work today is created digitally on a computer. He works out of his home studio in Central Florida with his wife Laura and a big, lazy, orange cat.

Try It Out!

Paint a clay pot in a Native American pattern!
Painting a clay pot with a Native American pattern is fun and easy. You can find samples of easy designs and patterns in the library or on the internet.

What You Need:
- Clean terracotta pots
- Acrylic craft paints in assorted colors
- Newspaper
- An old shirt or painter's smock
- Small artist's paintbrush

Steps:

1. Use acrylic paint. It won't wash out of clothes, but also won't flake off of a flower pot.

2. Cover your work area with newspaper, since acrylic paint is almost impossible to remove from some surfaces.

3. Wear an old shirt or smock that you don't mind getting paint on.

4. Set the terracotta pot upside down to make it more stable then begin painting.

5. Let your pot dry. Then, fill it with dirt and a favorite plant.